Fatty Cat

Written by
Simon Bruce Montgomery

Illustrated by
Alexandra Colombo

meadowside
CHILDREN'S BOOKS

There was a cat called Fatty Cat,
a big fat cat was he.

A really rather greedy cat,
as greedy as could be!

He'd eat macaroni, meat balls,
marzipan and mushy peas.
Burgers, baked beans, bolognaise
all topped with melted cheese!

Reluctantly he shared his house,
(which meant he shared his food,)
With a pair of crafty little mice,
whom he found rather rude.

These mice were always finding ways
to rob the cupboards bare
And Fatty Cat could never seem
to catch that sneaky pair!

One day the mice were licking clean
a plate of cherry pie
When Fatty Cat approached them
with a twinkle in his eye.

He'd come up with a cunning plan
to rid them from his lair
And stop them eating all the food

— the crafty little pair!

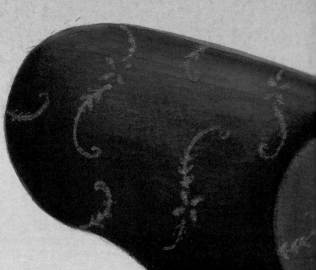

He told a very simple lie
he knew was sure to tease...

"Did you know that the moon is made **entirely out of cheese?**"

He didn't have to say it twice,
they dropped their spoons and ran!
To get themselves up to the moon,
they'd need a clever plan!

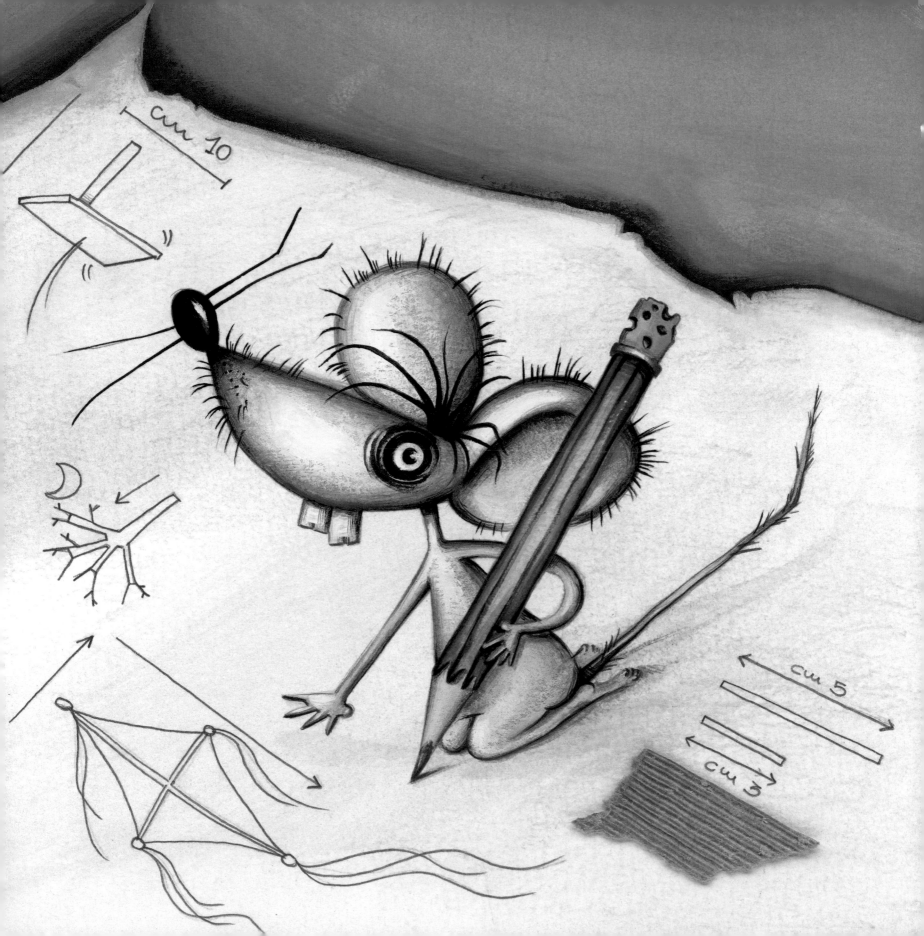

The wind just wasn't strong enough to fly the kite they found.

They built a tower of boxes, but it tumbled to the ground.

The trampoline seemed promising, but didn't do the trick...

They couldn't even reach it from a tree top with **a stick!**

Fatty Cat could not believe
his plan had worked so well.
He felt as if he'd cast a kind
of magic, cheesy spell.

Desserts were so much sweeter
with those greedy mice at bay,
and gleefully he sat back and
just watched them work away.

The days dragged on and still
the mice refused to take a rest.
It seemed that Fatty's trick had
made them totally possessed.

Then one night
after supper as he
made himself a treat,
He looked outside
and there it was...

...the Moon Machine, complete!

He watched them as they floated up
towards the moon-lit sky
And couldn't help but chuckle
as he waved them both goodbye!

One little fib and now the mice
were drifting far from home,
And Fatty Cat could once again
eat peacefully alone!

But one day during
breakfast something
landed on the mat,
A postcard that
had come from space
addressed to Fatty Cat.
And when he read out
what it said, he wasn't
too impressed...

"We thank you for the great advice…

this MOON CHEESE is **THE BEST!!!**"

To my wife, Kate,
for always believing
in my cunning plan

S.B.M.

For Pepi,
my big fatty cat

A.C.

First published in 2011
by Meadowside Children's Books
185 Fleet Street, London EC4A 2HS

www.meadowsidebooks.com

Text © Simon Montgomery 2011
Illustrations © Alexandra Colombo 2011

The rights of Simon Montgomery
and Alexandra Colombo to be
identified as the author and illustrator
of this work have been asserted by them
in accordance with the Copyright,
Designs and Patents Act, 1988

A CIP catalogue record for this book
is available from the British Library

1 2 3 4 5 6 7 8 9 10

Printed in China